WEST GRID STAMP

NN		RR		WW	
NT		RT		WO	
NC		RC		WL	
NH		RB		WM	
NL		RP		WT	
NV		RS		WA	
NM		RW	9b4	WR	
NB		RV		WS	
NE					
NP					

WITHDRAWN

Postman Pat
Plant Sitter

Scholastic Children's Books,
Scholastic Publications Ltd,
7-9 Pratt Street, London NW1 0AE

Scholastic Inc.,
730 Broadway, New York, NY 10003, USA

Scholastic Canada Ltd,
123 Newkirk Road, Richmond Hill,
Ontario, Canada L4C 3G5

Ashton Scholastic Pty Ltd,
PO Box 579, Gosford, New South Wales,
Australia

Ashton Scholastic Ltd,
Private Bag 1, Penrose, Auckland,
New Zealand

First Published by Scholastic Publications Limited 1993

Text copyright © 1993 by John Cunliffe
Illustrations copyright © 1993 by Scholastic
Publications Limited and Woodland
Animations Limited

ISBN 0 590 54001 7

Printed by PROOST, Belgium
Typeset by Contour Typesetters, London

Scholastic Publications Limited and Woodland
Animations Limited
All rights reserved

10 9 8 7 6 5 4 3 2 1

The right of John Cunliffe to be identified as the
author of this work has been asserted by him in
accordance with the Copyright, Designs and Patents
Act, 1988.

Story by **John Cunliffe**   *Pictures by* **Joan Hickson**

from the original Television designs by **Ivor Wood**

On Friday, Miss Hubbard said, "I'm going on holiday tomorrow."

"Lovely," said Pat.

"I'll need a plant-sitter," said Miss Hubbard.

"A what . . .?" said Pat.

"Someone to water all my plants. They'll die if no one takes care of them."

"I'll do it," said Pat.

"Good man," said Miss Hubbard. "Thanks."

"No trouble," said Pat. "I'll be calling, anyway, with the post."

Miss Hubbard showed Pat all her plants. He didn't know she had so many. There were plants in the sitting-room; plants in the kitchen; plants on the stairs; plants in the bedrooms; even plants in the toilet and bathroom.

"What a lot of plants!" said Pat.

"Listen," said Miss Hubbard. "This one needs watering once every three days. And this one's to be watered every day. This one needs plant-food once a week. If it's sunny, put this one in the shade."

Pat began to get muddled. He made notes on the back of an old envelope.

Miss Hubbard gave Pat a key.
"Have a good holiday," said Pat.

On Monday, Pat lost his notes about Miss Hubbard's plants.

"I'll give them all just a little sip of water," said Pat. "I expect they'll be all right."

On Tuesday, Jess's tail caught one of the plants. It fell off its shelf and the pot smashed on the floor.

"Oh, dear," said Pat. "What will Miss Hubbard say?"

He told Ted about this when he called with the letters.

"I've got hundreds of pots in the shed," said Ted. "Take your pick."

"Thanks," said Pat.

On Wednesday, Miss Hubbard's plants all began to droop and look sickly. Pat told Dorothy Thompson.

"They'll need a spot of plant-food," said Dorothy.

She lent him a bottle from the greenhouse.

17

"How much food did she say?" said Pat, on Thursday. "And which ones?"

He gave them all a drop.

On Thursday, Miss Hubbard sent a card for Pat. It said:

"*I hope my plants are well, I'm staying an extra week, so keep up the good work.*"

"Oh dear," said Pat.

On Friday, Miss Hubbard's plants looked much better. But Mrs. Goggins said, "You do look tired, Pat."

"It's these plants," said Pat.

Pat was delighted to see Miss Hubbard back from her holiday. He was ready for a rest from his plant-sitting.

"I've brought you a special present," she said, "to thank you for looking after my plants."

She brought out a large box.

What could it be?

Pat opened his present.

It was a plant. A large plant. A strange plant – such as Pat had never seen before.

"It will need looking after," said Miss Hubbard, "but you've had a lot of practice now."

"Yes," said Pat. "Thank you, Miss Hubbard."

When Sara saw Pat's present, she laughed and said, "You'll be entering the flower-show next."

"You never know," said Pat. "I might just do that."

Pat took good care of his plant. And he did put it in the flower-show. What a surprise for everyone! It won the second prize!

Miss Hubbard won the first prize, as she did every year.

"But," she said, "I had a wonderful plant-sitter. I'd never have won without his help. Thanks, Pat!"

"It's a pleasure," said Pat.